To my wife, Amanda. Every day with you is my luckiest day ever
- Mr. Jay

For Sue and Barry, for their love and support 6000 miles away
- Gary

New Paige Press, LLC
NewPaigePress.com

ISBN 978-1-7345980-3-2

Printed and bound in China

New Paige Press provides special discounts when purchased in larger volumes for premiums and promotional purposes, as well as for fundraising and educational use. Custom editions can also be created for special purposes. In addition, supplemental teaching material can be provided upon request. For more information, please visit NewPaigePress.com

TYRANNOSAURUS HEX

and the UNLUCKIEST DAY EVER

Written by
Mr. Jay

Illustrated by
Gary Wilkinson

In a dense patch of jungle, with the sun beating down,
lay Anda, the T-Rex, on the ground with a frown.

"What happened?" asked Bull, her dinosaur friend,
as playtime came halting to an unwelcomed end.

Injured and angry, and holding her knee,
Anda snorted, "I tripped - on the trunk of that tree."

"There's nothing to question, no reason to doubt,
that bad luck always follows when I'm out and about."

She got herself up and brushed herself off,
kicking up dust that caused her to cough.
"There's an ugly black cloud, floating over my head,
and I'd be better off staying in bed!" Anda said.

"So now what?" asked Bull, still wanting to play.
"It's too soon to go home on such a nice day."
But Anda stayed grumpy and in a bad mood,
"I guess we can hit the café for some food."

"A big scoop of ice cream will cheer you right up -
Blueberry Dream with nuts in a cup!"

Anda's mood brightened as they walked down the street, thinking about the great treat she would eat.

But the café was mobbed
with dinosaur kids,
and mammoths and turtles
and two wide-eyed squids,
who stood in a line
that seemed not to budge,
ordering mint chip and chocolate
and vanilla striped fudge.

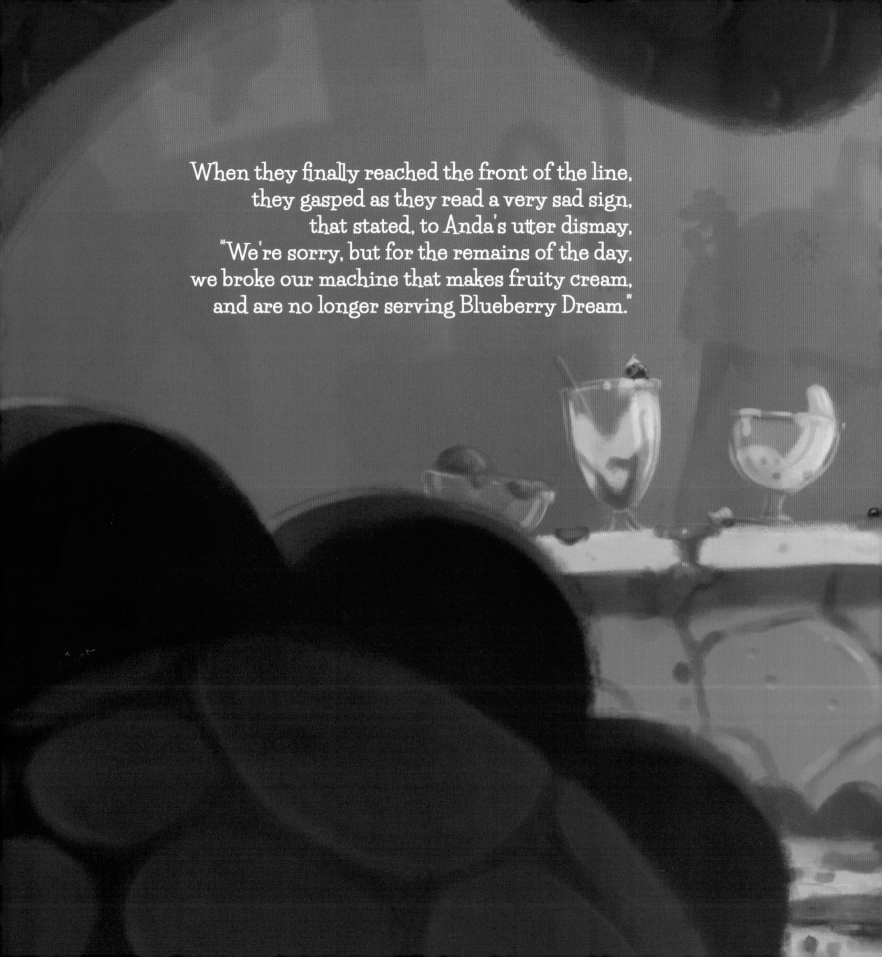

When they finally reached the front of the line,
they gasped as they read a very sad sign,
that stated, to Anda's utter dismay,
"We're sorry, but for the remains of the day,
we broke our machine that makes fruity cream,
and are no longer serving Blueberry Dream."

"More bad luck!" Anda stomped 'round and snorted,
her cheeks burning red and her features contorted.
"Come on, let's go home, this hex is a pain.
And oh, look at that - it's starting to rain!"

They walked toward her house, getting soaked 'long the way,
as Anda moaned on, "What a terrible day!"

Back in her kitchen, they had water and cake,
and Anda complained, "I cannot catch a break.
This terrible hex has run all amuck
and given me nothing but horrible luck."

Bull said, "Getting rid of bad luck
is a worthy objective,
and it's simply a matter
of changing perspective.
Let's think about all
that has happened today,
but let's look at it in
a more positive way:
You tripped and you fell -
it happens to all.
At one time or other,
we all take a fall.
But you got right back up -
it could have been worse -
so it's hard to believe
it was caused by a curse.

"And the café couldn't make your blueberry flavor,
but you could have then tried a *new* flavor to savor.

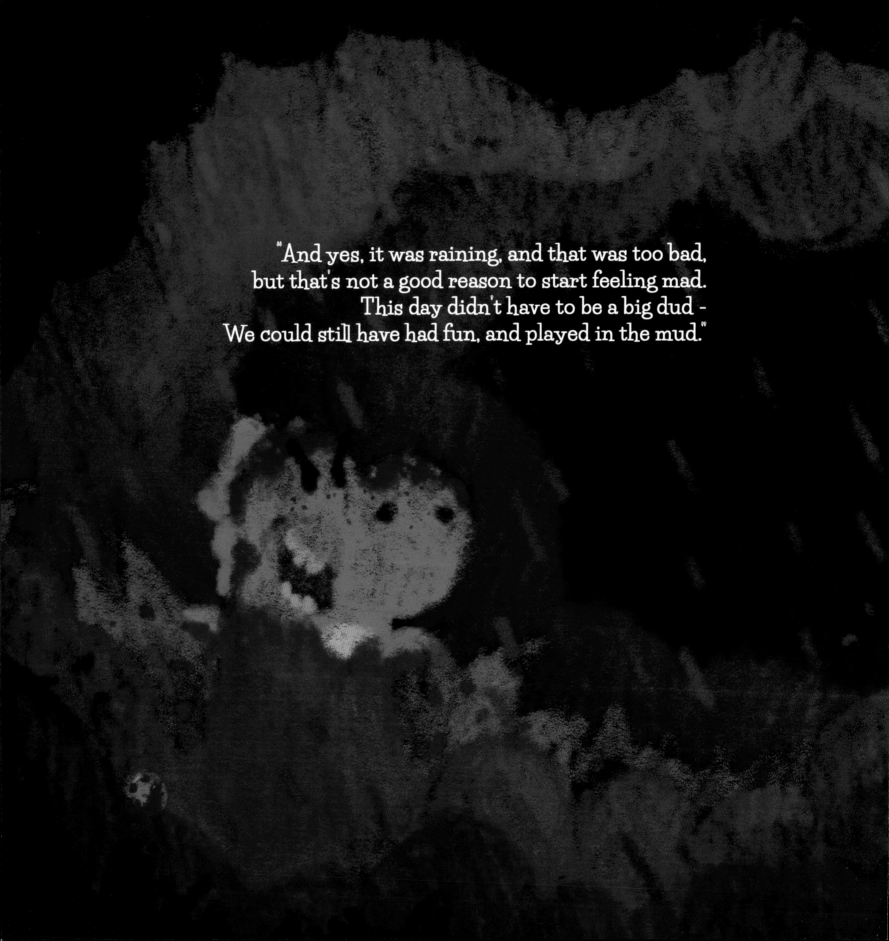

"And yes, it was raining, and that was too bad,
but that's not a good reason to start feeling mad.
This day didn't have to be a big dud -
We could still have had fun, and played in the mud."

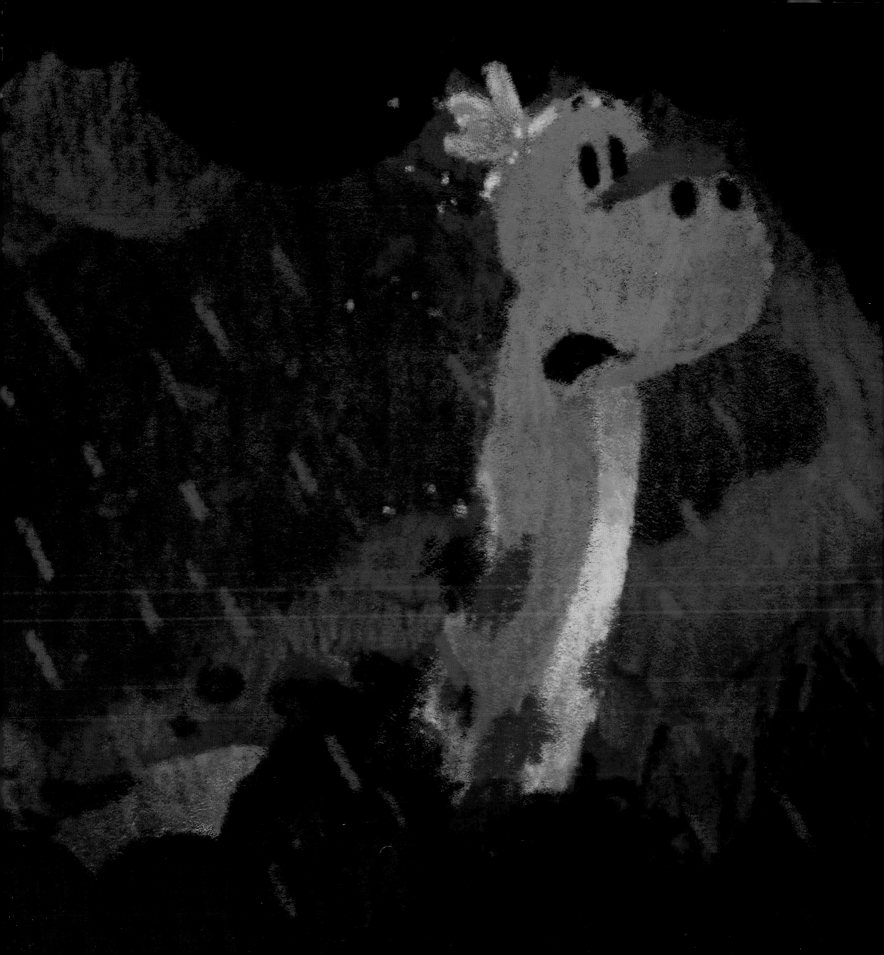

His words had made sense,
what he said sounded true,
perhaps all she needed
was a new point-of-view.
For a while they stayed quiet,
so Anda could think,
as Bull stood back up,
and went to the sink.

"I'll get you more water."
"No, thanks," she told Bull.
"For the very first time,
my glass is half full."